Written by Deb Smith

Published by Writers Block Publishing LLC

www.writersblockpublishingllc.com

Contents

Sing the Verses Out My Head

Deb Smith

Note from the Author:

This book has been a long time coming. My mother introduced me to poetry when I was a little girl. She was a writer as well. She took me to her poetry group meetings. She taught me to string words together into expressions of the world around me. Although she found solace in writing mostly religious inspirational poems, I discovered that writing was a way to vanquish the unspoken emotions on my mind. Writing became a cleansing ritual for me. A release of the thoughts that bubble over or eat me up inside. Most of my poems are fed by my own experiences but some are born of my observations woven with a creative yarn. All of them were vomited out of my spirit from a very personal place of reflection that necessary release. My hope is that in sharing my poems my readers will find those grains with which they can relate, smile those tickled secret smiles, laugh those knowing laughs, dry a tear, feel so not alone and relate to the awe and peace that I find in nature and spirituality. To some it may seem the musings of a mad woman. To me, I'm just singing the verses out of my head

Thank you
Please enjoy.

Deb

I dedicate this book to the memory of my mother and my two beautiful grandmothers who passed on to the other plain but still walk with me in my dreams and surround me with their love and guidance.
To my three wonderful sons and husband who support me.
To all the friends and loved ones who have encouraged me.
To the sun for always bathing me in its love and light and brightening up my days.

Haiku for the Rain

Glittering raindrops fall
Emotional mother
The sky is weeping

Haiku for the Red Moon

Wonder in obsidian sky
Triumphant crimson moon arises
Timeless eyes revere her beauty

Sage Song

With this smoke
I purify the atmosphere
I ask all negative energy to leave
All sadness, pain, familiar negative spirits, imprints of negative
energy leave
Do not return
There is no attachment for you here
I welcome positivity
Love, healing, blessing, abundance of wealth, peace and
positive drive
Energies of persons past leave
You are not welcome
This space is only open to loving ancestors here to help along
the way
This is a beautiful place of happiness and peace

Deb Smith

The Rug

I am a rug
With footprints on my back
Mud trampled into my matted hair
Soggy eyes
My face mashed
My tailbone stomped in
Cracked trampled ribs
Deflated spirit
Granulated confidence
An old thing kicked into a corner
Still holding on to a few wheezing breaths of life
Told it will get better
But how
I thought I was a warm blooded
Voluptuous
Vibrant
Vivacious
Voracious
Woman
I bat my eyes
I flipped my hair over my shoulders
I smiled with my teeth
And my lips
And my eyes
I strutted in heels
And socks
And bare feet
My hips felt good swaying to their own rhythm
My laugh trilled like a bell
My voice sang my self-assurance
Because I was loved
I had found it
It had found me and wrapped me like a present

It covered me with the warmth of a receiving blanket tucked in
tight at the corners
It gave me swagger
I bragged about its valor
It's everlasting care
Of me
But then
The ceiling caved
The bottom fell out
My alternate reality disintegrated
What I thought was real
Wasn't real at all
I wasn't loved
How could I be
My worship of you
Wasn't your worship of me
The scales fell from my eyes
I could finally see
Had I known
Deep in my bones did I suspect that I was not your Mary or Isis
or Nefertiti or Ra or Earth or Universe with rotating planets
galaxies and suns
You were that to me
I arose and set for you
I took in air to breathe for you
I walked
Talked
Worked
Hustled
Made a life and hearth and home
For you
And I
Was
Your
Rug
I'm in a corner
I'm crusty
Snot smeared from tears I can't stop
And I don't know what to do
Because I thought I was your woman
But that title belongs to many others

And I
Was just the rug

Egyptian Musk

Darlin you smell like an offering to the gods
If love was an essence
The fragrance would be your skin
It permeates my nostrils
Fills my lungs
Makes me cough with your fire
Your smoke
You are too hot to the touch
You burn through me
Your ash imprints to my bones
I am a vapor when you finish me
I melt back into a gas
Floating into the nothing
That I become
Without you
Awaiting the next episode
Of our
Mad Science

The Alter

I want to thank you for the offering of your body
Your giving selflessly
Of you exerting your strength and passion
Within me
Upon me
All over me
For your kisses so soft and tender
For your tongue so circling and seeking
Cleansing
Nourishing
Replenishing
I want to thank you for your religious dedication
To the church
Of this body
I am an offering
And you are the god receiving this gift in reception
To glorify and uplift
The passion and love that we share
Your gracious attentiveness to this flawed receptacle
This hallowed space
This creator of life
This baker of generations
This womb
For which you insert your
Healing vein
And anoint each stroke with
Blessed iniquity
Your service is precious
A communion
Take of your bread and my sacrificial blood
Eat and drink
To the oneness that we have achieved by the unity
Of two bodies connected
By flesh
And bone
And soul
And passion
And everlasting unity
Amen

Nocturnal Blindness

Sometimes the euphoria of the sex blinds us to the turd of shit
sitting in the middle of the floor
It's been there
Its crust hard and jagged
It's stink attracting flies
The rolling and writhing
The bouquet of fresh lust and musk fills the air
The moans and guttural inflections block out the sound of the
buzzing
The taste of momentary pleasure eludes the obvious
That the surroundings are horrible
The walls are bleak and dingy because no one bothers to make
this a home
A mirror hangs precariously from a rusted nail on one solitary
wall
Cracked and reflecting a portrait of the lovers
Two scribbles of confused matter fumbling in the dark
Searching for things that cannot be found
Absent fathers
Diminished self esteem
Self-worth
Pride
Control
Love
Healing
Filler for empty gaping holes
Bandages from past casualties
War veterans
Clawing
Pulling
Pushing
Desiring
Begging
Offering
Pleading
Stealing
Taking
Releasing
Only,

15

Deb Smith

To realize
Upon completion
The smell
That dingy empty room
The mirror reflecting two lumps of weary flesh
And a shit
A stinking shit
Still laying in the middle of the floor
Where does it end
When does healing begin?

Heartless Be Thy Name

Heartless
How could you sit there and watch me dying in front of you?
Shredding my heart methodically
Dissecting the ventricles
I bled out before your eyes
You left me a thing
Dull and ragged
Pulse lacking
Head lulling
Expected to take your harsh words and skip back to life
You gutted me
You took my carefully offered chalice and hocked into it
You knocked my golden offering to the ground and stamped
upon it for good measure
And laughed
Because my heartache is comical
To even me
A humorless laugh
My pea brain struggles to comprehend
Heartless
You know my existence lives on the punctuation of your every
word
Yet you keep silent
You keep me in limbo
Struggling with the void
Alone in the desolation
Frustrated with the sound of my own breathing
Wishing I could cry no more tears
I thought I was finished
I suffer in silence
What if I was to suffer no more
If I went into the dirt would you miss me
If I left this body and floated into the atmosphere like a gas would
you finally realize my worth
Without you there is no joy
I might as well become the dust
Cremate this pathetic bunch of bone, muscle and fat
Please let me cry no more

Deep, Deeper, Deepest

Part 1: Deep

Sassy sexy beast
Swing your hips
Cause you're sexy
Roll that body
Cause you're sexy
Bat those eyes
Cause you're sexy
Open those thighs
Cause you're sexy
Push up those boobs
Cause you're sexy
You can't feel
Cause you're sexy
Just wear high heels
Cause you're sexy
Wear a little dress
Cause you're sexy
You're a mess
Cause you're sexy
Wear red lips
Cause you're sexy
Don't let your heart slip
Cause you're sexy
You don't care
Cause you're sexy
You're just there
Cause you're sexy
Get replaced
You're not sexy
What a waste
You stopped being sexy
You're just a chick
Who thought she was sexy
Aw sexy beast
She ain't sexy

....
Part 2 Deeper

She's just some woman
In her off hours
She removes the liquid powder social mask and washes off her
disguise for the world
Her imperfections tatoo her skin
She looks less of a woman, more of a child
Baby face
Chubby
Little girl
Her hair on a hook in a room painted stark white holds nothing
back in the light of day
The curls of her mother and father and grandmother pile atop her
head in a full knot, a bun, a way to keep her thick unruly natural
bunch of hair out of her face
The grays mingle with the browns and the waves of the oceans
crossed by her ancestors fight the coils of the oppressed for who
is more prominent in texture
The white
The black
The native
They are all the same
It's just hair after all
The curve of her modest breasts ride averagely when they are
not coached to sit up and beg and stand at attention by Victoria's
little secrets cousin sold at the discount department store under
a more economical name
Maidenform's secret
Or maybe Bali's
Her belly talks of the children it has carried
Of the lives it has supported
Of the food it has devoured
Of the life it has lived strapped to the torso of a woman who
expresses her joy and pain through food or no food
Happy, give it more
Sad, give it more
Sad, give it less, I can't think about it
Happy, don't have too much I'm dieting again, gotta be sexy
Such an active part of her, yet it is her shame

19

Her shapely hips
She loves their curves as she poses in the mirror
They sashay to the time of a pendulum as she walks
The tooted out butt her mother slapped down in dresses
She knows is a highlight
"People pay money for butts like that, honey."
One Queenly acquaintance once told her
It sent her into fits of laughter
Her thick thighs are jingling baby
Her shapely legs could be shapelier, but she is lazy
Her favorite little feet
Her painted little toes
In the mirror is a golden brown woman
Her eyes blaze green and gray and sometimes a spot of brown
Hazel
Funny eyes some call them
"Are they yours?"
Yes, they are mine
"They are pretty."
I forget they are there…. Not really. But modesty is easier to
digest.
Her stature is not short but not tall
Medium
Average
She stares at the woman
In the mirror
The reflection
The body
The only woman she loves
She loves me
Sometimes
An average woman
This too is sexy
Birthday outfit just like Eve
A half smile curls up at the corner of her lips
For a quick second
Anybody watching
Would see a hint
Of the Beast
And still
She's underneath
The layers of the shell are dense

....
Part 3: Deepest

Dig deeper
Throw away the crane and the shovel and the trowel
Can't use your hands
Or your mind
Must use your heart
I am a woman
Dig down deep enough, it's all heart
I'm full of mush and softness and kindness and sweetness
I wear my feelings on my sleeves
When I pretend like I don't
It's just the old bullet ridden under armor
The protective mechanism
The thing I use to try to keep the real me safe but obviously
never safe enough
I'm hurt easily
The real me is a priceless mold of a woman made from hand-
blown glass
I have been broken and shattered many times
If you could see my spirit, you would be shocked at the amount
of duct tape and gobs of old dried glue and rusty bent nails and
thumb tacks and worn welded spots and blood stained yellowing
bandages and surgery stitching, some neat and barely visible,
some tacky like Frankenstein
All the times I have tried to piece myself back together after
someone has kicked a puss dripping open sore or turned a black
and blue bruise green or stuck their finger into a bullet hole and
poked or plucked the open unhealed flaps of my skin
I am a flawed woman
I can't declare that we are all flawed women
I only know the depths of me
And even as I say this, there are deep dark corners that I do not
allow myself entry
Not even I can go there because if I do, I know I will become lost
in the sorrow and murk and sludge and fetid feces of pain so
immense that it is better left to rot than to attempt to deal with it
It's too far gone
This is who I know myself to be
A woman who has been through the wars

21

Some of them I chose to fight in
For some I was drafted to fight in a battle I never asked for there to be
The glass woman
Begging to be loved
Begging to be treated with care
Begging for just one time where a chip is not cracked into my tender soul
One time where I am not bombed into shards
Standing with open arms again offering myself
Once again
To the experience of life

Dedication to Love

My love
In the silence of captured moments
In the quiet flashes of solitude that leave me to my own contemplation
In a state of meditation and repose
Your pensive brown eyes come to stare at me
For you are never far from my mind
When chaos fills to capacity the circumference of my complex soul
You are the calm that brings my mania to the river of peace
You are the oxygen that pumps into my heart and causes my lungs to breathe
How many times have you resuscitated me
You are my healing vain
You are the salve upon the chronic unnamed pain within my soul
You are my joy
My laughter
The hands that lift me up and dedicate me to the sky
Under your wings I feel the warmth of the sun
You are my sunshine
The warm glow upon my golden skin
My daily rainbow after the storm and rain
You are my strength
You are my rock
You are my happy
You are my smile
You are my pleasure
You are my pain
You are my love
To our united star in the expanse of the dark night
Under the shadow of the moon's protection
I acknowledge your name
And whisper its confirmation to the universe
My love
My love
Over and over
Again
My love

Unadulterated Bliss

For my every waking moment
My mind conjures your face
My dreams are overwhelmed with only you
Violets and lavender kisses
Sunlight and warmth
Smother me with your essence
Roses and Daylilies
Because this beauty is like a moment in your arms
A second between your lips
The fragrance of love making
When fucking is in bloom
A garden nurtured by sweet sweet seduction
The depth of which brings us alive
I awaken from your touch
I live by the stroke of your confessions to my womb
Deep cave
Accept this traveler who seeks to find himself
Rejuvenate him
Give him rest
The healing waters overflow
Make him a part of me
We are now one
Unity and circles linked in copper chain
We will rust and bleed together
Fused from the same fire eternal
Ethereal we are connected
Dwelling inside a vacuum of our own space
A garden
Outside of time immortal
Existence ignited inside two eyes
One filled with earth
One a globe of trees and gray skies
We collide and make rain
See my love, we are everything
We ever needed
In the real world
Before we open our eyes to the apparition
We are perfect

Sing the Verses Out My Head

Keep your eyes closed
Stay inside
I will hold you tight
We are perfect

Him & Me

His voice is like
Smooth warm chocolate
Melted on a rock
On a sweltering hot day
Like umm I want to dip my fingers in
Take a taste
Get myself a little messy
Along the way
Hypnotized by the words he says
Can't get his voice out my head
Sweet oil pouring into my ears
Lubricates my mind
Calms my inner fears
And he
Been doing this trick for years
Connected
Like bellybuttons and umbilical cords
He nourishes me on the inside
Buckle up my saddle let me take a ride
Buck on the bronco
Then take it smooth and glide
Lay me on my side and slide slide slide
Caramel kisses
On the bottom lip
Makes my whole consciousness slip
I mean, who am I really
I can't remember
Is this that Juju
I surrender
OOO! Hot peas and butter pound cake
His vibrations resonate
Electric currents down to my curled toes
Exactly what this Goddess needs only he knows
This brotha gives me arrhythmia as far as love goes
Addicted
He is my drug I don't need to sniff nothing up my nose
Caught in the viewfinder of those baby browns
I am froze

He sees straight through me like I'm not wearing a stitch of
clothes
He makes me feel naked
And beautiful
And glistening
Like a buttercup in a field of wildflowers
Sweet
Precious
One of a kind
I rub my petals against his skin and make him glow
I close my eyes
Meditate and stalk his dreams
He wakes up smiling from fantasies of me
We are in tune, One touch
I'm on an electric current bound for the moon
I can't wait to be with him soon
It's timeless this thing of ours

Familiar Spirits

Innocence left me by the door
At the age of four
When my mother
Indoctrinated me into the world of women's heartache
I was too young
But it was done
And the lesson was
That men hurt
And women cry
I'd sit and wipe the tears from her eyes
I was too young
But momma never lied
And though she's gone
Sometimes
I feel her within my own hiccupping sobs
My own personal pain
Also caused by a man
Here we are again
Me and momma
One the side of the bed
Crying for heartbreak
And innocence lost
I was too young
But momma knew there'd be days
Was it premonition to teach me the ways
Or a curse
Love hard
Get treated in reverse
Sit alone sick heart and nurse
Momma knew there'd be days
I wish she wasn't psychic
I wish things were different.

Insomnia, How My Chemicals Speak

Sing the verses out of my head
Give me peace
Release
Silence
Maybe I can sleep
Anxiety be still
I'm fighting to have the will
Depressed
Can't stop thinking
No help from the drinking
My mind is racing
Rest is evasive
I no longer like me
Brain please stop fighting
Let me be calm
I'm up till dawn
And I just can't stop
Singing the verses in my head
Humming
Hmm mmm mmm mmmm mmm
Rock yourself Baby, it will feel better

Where Does the Truth Lie

In the absence of truth
We tend to glorify our memories
The memorized moments
Formulated into false realities that live only within the expanse of
our lofty minds
It didn't really happen like that
But within our truth we have made it so
We glorify people who never did exist
We create our own interpretation of the events, long after the
events, because this turn of events makes us happy
It makes us the hero
It takes the nasty
The putrid and the painful things and renders a memorized past
of an existence in la-la land
A heaven of our own minds spun with a surreal artists twist into a
place that never did exist
My mind says it happened this way and as I overthink the
replayed film viewing in my head
I cut
And cut
To the editing floor go the splices and dices that have made me
into this picker of daisies in a field skipping along through a sick
reality that I was forced to live through that I chose not to
remember any more
No!
You can't make me open that door
That pandora's box
See I have it blocked
Out of my cerebral cortex
These manifestations of my own imagination
Are the truth
Because I said so
And you
You can't tell me no
They are mine
Because I said so
I am living my truth
No matter how false it seems to you
This is my survival technique

Sing the Verses Out My Head

And I
Am still living
That's truth

Happy

My loves eyes are brown vast like the sands of a desert basking
in the sun
I can go on for days
Pacing in circles
Lost in the depth of their
Ethereal beauty
My loves voice
Clear as a bell
Deep like the hum of a monk's chant over and over in my ears
does ring
He is calling out to me to draw me into him
Where I live within his large heart
My spirit knows him
Whether he speaks with his lips or the currents of his intelligent
brain I know that voice it says
You
You are mine
I know you hear me calling you
You are mine
I am yours
She his
He hers
We are we
And us
Well, we are something special
Damn special
We are linked by the cords of time and destiny
Unbreakable impenetrable connection
A unity that we share
When we hold us, we operate as if no one else is there
Off we spiral into the air
My love and me
We rotate
Around the sun moon and stars
Past mars
We make our own planet
We call it
Well, we can't tell you what we call it
But you can call it

Shangri-La
We call it
Happy

Longing for Stolen Moments

I wish for the snow
Clean
Cold blanket covering all that can be seen
With pure
Pretty
Winter
Peaceful
Nothingness
Silence
After the first falling
The crunch of foot fall
Innocence in breath blowing into smoke
Condensation
The stars
The silence
And my hand
Slipping into yours
Fingers entwined
In a moment
Of pristine
Elysium

Breakfast

Waking up to love
Golden sunlight peeks through curtain shade
Your lips brim with a smile I bless them with a kiss
Soft silky velvet paradise
Feathery lashes flutter against my cheek
Our eyes remain closed
The better to see each other
Our fingers find the places that memory knows so well
Your fingers trace my round curves
Mine graze in a forest of course hair
Arms
Chest
We explore the secret places
The places for which we have branded each other's names
Mine
Yours
Yours
Mine
We dine the feast of the passionate
Giving more and more until full
Bursting with satisfaction
And then
We lay basking in the glow of glistening sweat
Our parting favor
Of early morning love

Deb Smith

We Have Become

Missing a memory
A ghost walks by wearing your old expression
Whispers on the wind
Sing the haunting sounds of broken promises
It was never meant to be
Forever
Never
In my wildest dreams would I have ever imagined your eyes
would find me a stranger
I'm just a woman
You're just a man
The pregnant silence is more than either of us can stand
Once we couldn't shut up
There was so much to tell
Your words
Tagged my words
Tagged in your words
My smile
Caused your smile
And now
I don't trust the molecules in the air you breathe
And you have no use for me
I don't know what we're doing
We
Have come undone
Where once we were two
Us
Now
We seem to be
One
And
One
Which makes us
None
Done
Oh God, are we done?

I Am

I
Am the fire that burns deep within
A Jinn
An avatar
Woman
I am not
Essence of her life force
I am
The energy that gave this puppet the first day
I
Am never afraid
My knowledge comes from far away
I am older than Dogon traditions, the Mayan pyramids, the ruins
of Nubia
I taught the ancients how to pray
I am from before
Before the heat and the ice
Before the heat and the ice
Before the heat and the ice
The cycle repeats
I
Am never ending
Intellectual minds call me the soul
But they do not know
My origins
I have no origins
I have always been
I will always be
Goddess omnipotent
I expose myself in dreams
Clairvoyant
I know all things
I am the sixth sense
I am your Deja vu
I am the you
Within you
And we are all inside
The eternal

Deb Smith

The universe none can comprehend
We are
Thee
I am

Instructions Included

Tell me I'm beautiful
An unsolicited declaration
Just because
You
Think I am
Tell me you love me
Shock me into a blush
A silent smile
The revelation unexpected
Warmth spreads from my cheeks
To my heart
Float butterflies in my belly
A river in my gully
Tell me the things that make me glad I am a woman
And glad you are a man

Deb Smith

Gone in An Instant

As the blood trickled down my leg
I knew she was gone
He was gone
The life not yet a life was leaving
Retreating
Baby did you take a peek
Before you came down to see
That this life is a hard kernel of existence
You wanted no part of this
You chose to resist this
Death sentence
From birth till who knows when
Fighting over and over again
Day by day a struggle
A war and a hustle
Trying to just stay alive
The hell of trying to survive
Facing the cruel world
Day in day out
Makes me want to throw up my hands and shout
Please go
Don't come
It's ok
I wouldn't want you to suffer anyway
It's harder for the children of today
Let the cleansing blood flow
I love you but go
Miscarry now
Verses face a miscarriage of life
Where there is no future
At least not in the way
I would wish it for you
Don't come my little bird
I'll take on the pain
Dripping down my leg
Isn't this life full of confusion

Lost and Confused

You never leave my mind
Although if one were to examine the contents of yours
Traces of me would scarlessly be found
A single curly hair
A hint of a hazel eye
Do you know my eyes are hazel?
What do you remember?
It's been so long
Am I desirable to you still?
I don't feel like a thing of beauty without your eyes on me
That way
Do you look through me?
Am I not the thing that moves your body to desire?
I haven't changed
Maybe that is the problem
Is there a problem?
Things are confused
Do I have to become another thing for you to want me?
Why can't I be just this woman
Why can't you be just this man
My heart
My soul
My spirit
My skin
All 7 of my chakras
My Orishas and ancestors on my behalf
We are all confused
Because the stars and the planets aligned and gave us their
permission and their grace
But we are down here making a mess of things
I'm not a mess
I'm reacting
Or that is what I will stand by
Reaction to your actions
What are we doing with this life?
But we won't remember the next
Is this our track record

Is this what we do
You hurt me
I chronically feel hurt by you
What is this cycle
I'm stuck on a rollercoaster that never ends
Same thing
Same behavior
Over and over
Again
Yet I'll die if it ever ends
I am a glutton for punishment
I must be a masochist
Sadistic
Unconsciously you do these things
Are you ever aware of what it does to me?
You can't be that blind
You want your cake and to eat it too
But I am not a dessert
I am a woman
And I want to know
Do you still see me?
Because I feel invisible
My heart
Do you still see me?

Songs of My Depression

What is it to suffer in silence?
The truth is no one really cares
I am the darkness, in the quiet
You look around and no one is there
Eyes glazed in space of dusk light
Fingers pulling at curls of tangled hair
All beings go on with their lives
Yet you are suspended in dank air
Is this fair
Or deserved
Truth be told maybe it's penance for my sins

PTS Me

The past has done a job on me
I'm damaged goods
Every new experienced causes a shiver
A shielding of my person
An attempt to protect my bruised shell from another beating
A shattering of spirit
Another one of life's tough love lessons to injure my resolve and
render my confidence a withered thing that is as tender as a leaf
I want to reach from behind the shell and extend my hands into
the light
I long for the warmth
For the good to caress my skin
To be embraced in love
To dance in the glow of carefree happiness
I extend a toe
I slide out from the shadows of my pain and regret
I stand under the stars and beg them to come down and ignite
me
Give me life
Bathe me in red and blue and green and gold
I want to fly into the expanse of the air and feel the beauty of the
wind against my skin
I want to be healed
I want to be free
But when I open my eyes, I see the same old thing
Overwhelmed by anxiety

Requiem of a Storm

The clouds are clearing their throat
Grumbling
Rolling thunder
The trees are waving their massive arms to and fro
The wind is shouting into the air
The rain showers the land with no abandon
Spontaneous light ignites the sky
A mist covers the earth as far as can be seen
Strange birds eek and fly quickly
In a way it is silent
In a way it is peaceful
In a way it is curious and foreboding
Was it this way in the beginning
Of things
In nature and the worlds innocence
The dance of the elements
The call of the uncontrollable
Man can't schedule or control this
Storms are rogue
Beautiful in their wildness
A sight to behold
The cool air as it ebbs
The peace as it calms
In the essence of a storm
Is the amazing handiwork of a powerful God

Unhinged

Unhinged
The snow looked beautiful
I wanted it to envelop me
I wanted to steal its peace
Some of its silence
It was too pure
Untouched
And I
Too full of silent turmoil
If I touch it will it make me peaceful too
Or will I ruin it
I stepped out into the snow in my bare feet
The cold whipped around my body
I felt nothing but cool air
Gingerly I stepped
Making footsteps in the virgin snow
I was timid at first
I turned to study them
Barely there
As am I
I want to be
I want to matter
In a daze of my off-beat chemicals
I went and lay by a warm body
He commented on my cold feet
They were numb to me
He covered me with wool and stuffing
But this was not the covering I needed
He looked at me
I looked off
Thinking of the snow
Longing for internal peace
He rubbed and scratched my back
I thought peace had come to me
But it always stops too short
Always left wanting
The snow would have me
I would go back to the snow
I grabbed a sweater

Maybe sense was returning
I saw the snow through the glass
It was still waiting
To welcome me
As I slid back the glass the wind blew a welcoming breath
It tingled on my ankles
I stepped out into the cold peace
I made footprints until I couldn't feel my feet anymore
And then sadly I stepped back inside
I was real for seconds in a life
I pressed play on my phone
Debussy's Clair de Lune

Home Free

In the quiet of the late afternoon
I sat in the ebb of waning sunlight
Relishing the breeze caressing my sensitive skin
It tickled the strange blonde hairs on my brown arms
I watched the shadow of light move ever so slightly like sheaves
of wheat in a meadow
My freckles, like my father before me, awaken and reveal
themselves with the encouragement of the sun
I stretch my shapely legs and wiggle my chubby little toes
I feel free and relaxed after a hard day of worshipping the
corporate god
The soul sucking corporate god
I close my eyes and hear the birds conversing in their ancient
tongue
This moment is the essence of free.

In the Eye of the Beholder

The scratch of beard beneath my fingertips
The bulge of Adam's apple against my lips
Forest of chest hair
Softness of belly
My pleasure
My pleasure
The center of my pleasure
Powerful legs
Arms that wrap me tight
Hands that touch me just right
Eyes that bore through my soul
Man who makes me whole
I've seen every crevice
Every mole
The beauty secreted within this soul
My feet are planted
My heart secured
You decide how to keep me, I'm yours.

Dreams of Nourishment When Hungry

Smothered by my warmth and wet
Strawberry sweet
Peach blossoms
Dripping
The nectar of desire
Decades of wonder
Premonitions lead to satisfaction
Passions revealed
Deep deep within my cavern
Our desires unfurl
And we
Ride each other
Like torrid waves on the ocean
Swim within these deep waters
Drown to the bottom of my sea
Find the golden treasure
Waiting
To be set free
Inside me
Give me release
Unleash me

Missing Mother

I am an adult woman who misses her mother
When the man who took me from her more than half my life ago
is not sensible and I feel there is no one to help me
No one to hold me when I just need some comfort and a good
cry
I'm an adult woman who misses her mother
They say she is with the angels
They say with God
But to me it feels like she was put into the earth to disintegrate
into food for bugs
I am alone to find my way in these so far unchartered waters
When my children are grown, and I don't know how to guide
them further
I am an adult woman who misses her mother
So, you've bore me and left me
There's no one to laugh with about the things that seem
devastating in the moment but may blow over
There's no one to hold my hand or dry my tears and tell me it will
be ok
There is no one to hug me and give me a shoulder when I just
need to be held
When I feel sick and tired of being sick and tired, I sit alone with
my tears and snot and the sounds of my own sniffling
I just want someone to love me unadulterated
I miss my mother's love
I am an adult woman who misses her mother
But when she walked the earth this was not what she gave to me
She gave me the view of her sorrow as she was misused and
abused by my father
She made me her confidant and comforter at an early age
I wiped her sorry tears
She taught me to stay even when everything seems wrong
She taught me to live in pain until the end
She taught me that only she was important
That her hugs to me were for her own benefit
She taught me that it was her way or the highway
She taught me the definition of a narcissist

She showed me envy for my little bit of escape
She showed me jealousy for the things I learned to take for
myself, but she never demanded of herself
She showed me silence when I needed her most
And just before it was too late, she gave me her pathetic love
and then left
The truth is that
I am an adult woman who misses the pieces of her mother that
were good and the others I can do without
I am an adult woman who realizes that her mother was a flawed
creature and yet I loved her still
I am an adult woman who misses this human being
A woman
Who gave birth to me
And raised me for several years
But she was no saint
Because saints aren't real
And sometimes I wonder
Was my mother ever real
Because I can't feel her
And I miss what was her
And even if they weren't perfect, I miss her arms
And even though she wasn't perfect, I miss her dearly
For the past 13 years, I've been an adult woman who misses her
mother
26 years since I have myself become a mother
43 years since I left the nurture of her womb
An infinity
Mommy, I miss you.

<u>Aaron</u>

My beautiful boy
Smile ignites my heart brighter than the sun
My son
My heart
My reason for living
When I was 17 years old
Honestly, he chose me
People said I was too young
I couldn't be a mother
But my heart said
I am empty
There's plenty of space
To fill
With this choice
I realized
I was chosen
Maybe by God
Maybe by the divine fate of the universe
Maybe by myself yearning for someone to love me
But definitely
By a soul
Who chose to come and bring wholeness
To a broken young girl
And for the rest of my life
And his
I am honored that he calls me mother
And I am grateful
That in the ethereal complex miracle of creation
He looked down through the stars
Or through the nebulae
Through the expansive bosom of God
And chose to be born of me
Thank you
Thank you
Tears of joy
For my beautiful boy

For the Love of Music

True love is like a song
With each beat of a full heart
The drums calling the souls back to the obsidian rich soil
Bursting with diamonds glistening like fresh water
Gold sparkling like the sun of a woman's smile
Her opulent oil secreted down within her deepest places
True love is like home
Love is like Africa
Like our mother land
Love is like our mothers
Warm nurturing hands to swaddle us
Full breasts to give us life
True love is like music
With lips that caress ever so softly
And spring forth the memory of the first time lips touched your
skin and ignited your soul
Its sweetness quenching the scorched fires within
True love is like a river
With crystalline waters that carry you to an oasis of peace
A reservoir in the desert of life
True love is like a song
The melody of two people dancing closer than closer than one
person dancing alone on a dance floor if that dance floor was on
a musical note
And the chorus was a mantra
And every lyric a meditation
True love is music itself
Music being the ultimate God created expression of love
It is humming
It is scatting
It is jazz
It is blues
It is the song that never needs sung because we already sing it
each time our bodies collide into each other and make
Beautiful music
Music is a love song
It needs no words

Sing the Verses Out My Head

No verse
It just needs
You
And me
And the instinctive tribal beat of our hearts

Deb Smith

A Song for Today

An end of an era
A closing of doors
Preparation for new journeys
Bittersweet
Nervous joy
As the past opens its arms
I am free
The sky is vast and blue
Shyly I spread my wings
Little brown bird soaring into
Possibility

Sing the Verses Out My Head